You are Amazing

A Collection of Inspiring Stories about Friendship,
Courage, Self-Confidence and the Importance
of Working Together

Nadia Ross

Special Art Stories

You are Amazing

A Collection of Inspiring Stories about Friendship, Courage, Self-Confidence and the Importance of Working Together

Nadia Ross

PAPERBACK ISBN: 979-12-80592-90-3

support@specialartbooks.com
www.specialartbooks.com

Table of Contents

Introduction

Hello, Boys and Girls!

The world is a very special place, and it's all because you are in it! Even when things seem like they will be hard, do you know you can still pull through? Especially if you are working together. Teamwork and forming friendships with others help make the world a better place.

Having someone at your side will also give you a chance to feel supported, loved, and cheered on during good times and times that are not so good.

Remember that the world will give you a chance to show all you can do. Boys and girls, don't shy away from these moments. Find what makes you unique and dig deep to discover additional parts of yourself that you didn't know were there. You just have to believe in yourself.

There will be times when you think something isn't possible, but you can go far beyond with the right attitude, support, and help from your friends! I created the stories in this book for you. They will help you find inspiration in small and big moments. These are boys and girls who have problems and fix them. They have challenges and face them— even when they are sad or scared—and they prove they can do anything when they just try.

Bella & Her Bully

Have you ever come across someone who was furious and talked to you in a naty way? Maybe they even bullied you, and you didn't know why? You are not alone. Sometimes, people get angry or sad, and they don't know what to do with their feelings.

And, instead of thinking about it and finding a different way to feel them, they react and may hurt someone's feelings, too. This way isn't nice when treating others. It doesn't make anyone feel good.

Let's find out how our main character, Bella, handles her bully and see what choices she makes.

~ ~ ~

Bella was sitting in class, cleaning out her desk. She liked to keep things organized to find what she needed quickly and easily. She took her books, then her pencils, then her folders, and placed them on the top of her desk. When she sat up, she saw three boys standing in front of her, and the tallest boy named Josh took her pencils and knocked them onto the floor.

"Why would you do that?" Bella asked in a curious tone.

"Because I'm sick of you always cleaning your stuff up. You don't need to, yet you do it every day. Now, I gave you a reason to clean up your stuff." Josh said. He flipped over her books and took out the papers from her folder.

The other two boys laughed at Josh as he made a mess of her things.

"I don't think that it hurts you in any way," Bella said. Even though she was a little frustrated at what Josh was doing, she still spoke to him calmly. She stood and picked up her pencils from the floor. Then she placed them back in the box. "Also, I don't think what you are doing is very nice. I wasn't paying any attention to you. You should leave me alone."

"Oh?"

"Yes, please."

Josh laughed and said, "Well, I made my point. Now you can clean up a bigger mess that actually needs your attention." He turned around, and his two friends followed him back to their side of the room.

None of her homework and worksheets were ripped or dirty, but she didn't like that someone came over and messed up her stuff and didn't think it was right for them to do it.

Bella wondered what she could do to stop it from happening?

When Bella went home from school that day, her older brother, Billy, noticed that she didn't talk as much as she usually did. While Bella was never the kind of sister who yelled and screamed, she had a happier way of looking at life and often had a smile on her face. Today, though, she was not smiling. Her eyes looked down, and her shoulders seemed to slump.

Billy knew they got along very well, and if something was bothering her, he wanted to help. So he asked his younger sister, "What is going on, Bella? Did you have a bad day at school?"

Bella bit her lip. She wasn't sure what to say about what had happened yet. Josh and his friend's actions confused her and hurt her feelings, but she didn't want to talk about it. Instead, she just shook her head no and said, "I'm just tired." She went into her room and closed the door. Billy went to knock on it but heard her sit down on her bed and thought maybe she would take a nap.

He went down to his mom, who was making their after-school snack, and said, "I think Bella is sad about something. I asked her, and she said she was tired."

"Well, that's very nice of you to be worried about your little sister. But maybe she just needs a rest, or maybe she needs some time to think about things, and she will come to you later."

Billy crunched into his apple and thought about what his mom said. She was pretty smart when it came to kid stuff, so he nodded his head and said, "Okay. I will wait until she talks to me about it." He finished up his snack, put his plate in the sink, and went to do his homework.

The next morning, when they were getting ready for school, Bella seemed to be feeling better. Billy

guessed she was tired and decided to forget about yesterday.

But after lunch, Billy saw Bella sitting with her friends on a bench. Each of the girls had a book they were reading when the three boys came up to them. Josh pulled the book out of Bella's hands and started flapping it around her head.

Billy was worried by what he saw. He didn't like the way the boy was talking to his sister, and he walked up to the group of kids and make sure that Bella was okay, but he stopped. He saw Bella

11

hold her hand out and just sit there. She was quiet and didn't blink, but after a few moments, the tallest boy rolled his eyes, said something else, and placed the book back into her hand.

Billy watched his younger sister and wondered what he should do. Now, he could pretend that he hadn't seen the tall boy bullying his sister, but then he could also talk to her about what he saw. Billy thought for a moment and asked himself what would make him feel better?

In the end, he realized that asking Bella about the bully would make him feel like he was doing his job as an older brother. If she said she didn't want to talk about it, he wouldn't push her to, but just putting himself out to her would help.

When they got home, and after their snack, Billy made his way toward Bella's room. When he got there, he knocked on her door and waited until she said, "Come on in!" Billy was feeling a little nervous when he opened her door, so he remained in the doorway for a moment.

"Hi, Billy. What's up?" Bella said, turning to him. She didn't look sad today, which made Billy feel better, so he took a deep breath and said, "I saw

that tall kid take your book today. Is there any-thing you want to talk about?"

Bella motioned for him to sit on the bed. She closed the door and sat next to him. "I'm not sure what to do. That tall boy is named Josh, and he just came over to me yesterday and started knocking things off of my desk. He said that I was always clean-ing when I didn't need to and that he was giving me a reason to do it. And today, you saw what happened."

Bella continued, "The problem is that I don't think he is a mean boy. I could tell about him, but I don't think that would do anything except make him feel more lonely. He wants to be organized, and he wants to read books. I'm just not sure if that is right. His friends seem angry, and I also thought about having you and your friends scare them to leave me alone." Billy smiled at that because he liked that his younger sister had thought about coming to him for help. He would protect his sister if he had to. "But that wouldn't help Josh, either. I just don't know. I wouldn't say I like it when he picks on me, but I can tell that he is picking on me for a reason. I'm just having a hard time making a choice."

"I'm glad you talked to me about it!" Billy said a little too happily. He was relieved that his sister was okay and comfortable talking to him. "So, you have two choices, right?" Bella nodded. Billy laid them out for her. "You could talk to a grown-up about it. Talk to Josh about it." Billy laughed at the idea but already knew what choice Bella would make, so he asked, "What choice would make you feel best about yourself?"

Bella thought for a moment and then said, "I would like to talk to Josh first and away from his friends."

"Then you should do that."

Bella hugged her brother and said, "Thank you. I should have come to you sooner."

"Well, you know for next time." They hugged and came up with a plan for the next day.

Before school, Billy and his friends went up to Josh and his friends and distracted the friends by just talking to them.

Bella snuck up as Josh looked on and tapped him on the shoulder. "Can we talk?" she asked.

Josh stuffed his hands into his pockets and looked back at his friends, who were talking to the older boys, and said, "Yeah. I guess so."

They walked away from the group, and then Bella asked, "Why are you picking on me?"

Josh blinked. He was surprised she just came up and asked him, but said, "You are always doing something. I get frustrated because I can't think of things like that. You always seem to have a book, and I was jealous to see how good you are at organizing. I don't know how to do any of that."

"Why don't you let me help you?" Bella said.

"You would help me?" Josh asked.

"Yes. I don't like that you are picking on me, and I didn't like that you knocked all the stuff off of my desk, but if you want help thinking of fun things to do or even cleaning out your desk, I can help."

Josh rubbed his hands through his hair. "Oh. Gee. I'm sorry. I didn't realize all I had to do was ask."

"Well, now you know for next time," Bella said and smiled, thinking about Billy.

Bella knew after that she had made the right choice and was very proud of herself. Maybe, Bella thought, in the future, she and Josh might even become friends.

~ ~ ~

When you are unsure and can't decide about something, talking to the people who love you most can help make your decision easier. They will be the people who help guide you through life's challenges. Don't be afraid to stand up for yourself and talk to someone who makes you feel bad. Even if they don't mean to hurt your feelings, they may just be looking for a friend to talk to.

Tony & His Activities

When people have a lot of spirit, they do many things to keep themselves busy. But, even though the person is having fun taking part in all their activities, they can run out of time to be around those who love them the most.

Finding time to do the things we love and still create time for those we love can be hard. But, by shaking things up and making space for everyone they are close to, they can find enough room for everything.

Tony and Tabitha are brother and sister. Find out how they overcome this struggle by working together, listening to each other, and letting love guide their way.

~ ~ ~

Tony and Tabitha woke up on a Saturday with different ideas about what they wanted to do. Tabitha was ready to spend the morning with her brother, playing in the creek behind the house like they often did when the weather was still warm.

They would look for rocks and crayfish, find frogs, and study the wildlife. They both liked science! Tony had to rush to eat breakfast and then go to his baseball practice, which he was excited about. Then, after practice, he had to start building a rocket for his science club.

They got up and dressed and made their way down to the breakfast table. Tabitha noticed Tony was dressed for baseball practice. She became very disappointed and said, "I didn't know you had practice today. I thought we could play in the creek out back."

Tony shook his head. "Sorry, Tabitha. I don't have time today. I have the stuff to do for the science

club, and my practice is probably going to be about two hours."

"Two hours!" Tabitha said. She groaned, but Tony didn't realize because he loved playing baseball so much and hanging out with his friends. He finished eating, put his plate in the sink, and hugged his sister. "I'll see you later. We'll try to go to the creek in the afternoon, okay?"

Tabitha nodded, but was still sad. She couldn't believe how busy Tony had become with all his activities lately. She could sense he was forgetting all the fun times they used to have together.

20

While Tony was at practice, Tabitha had a hard time finding things to do by herself. She realized maybe she didn't like being home without her brother, and she went to talk to her dad.

"Hi, Dad," Tabitha said.

Her dad put down his pen and looked at her. "Hey, Tabitha. How is your Saturday going?"

She pulled up a chair to sit next to him and rested her chin on her hand. She slumped over because she was a little sad. "It's not good. I miss Tony. I didn't know he was going to practice today. And then he has the stuff to do for the science club. He's finding so many activities to do. What if he forgets all about me?" she said.

Tabitha's dad placed his hand on her shoulder and said, "Oh my sweet girl, he will not forget about you. You are his most favorite person in the world. We can do two things to make you feel better about this. The first you can do is talk to Tony. Tell him you miss him and ask him to make some special time for just the two of you. The second thing we can do is start looking at activities for you to do. That way, you can learn more about a topic

you are interested in, burn some energy, and keep having fun, too."

Tabitha thought for a moment. Both options sounded good. She was also happy to hear that she was her brother's favorite person. Tony was her favorite person, too, and she hoped it would always stay that way.

"Thank you, Dad," Tabitha said, and she stood up to hug him.

"You are welcome." He pulled back and said, "Now, what kind of activity do you want to try?"

Tabitha spent a little while longer talking with her dad. They planned out how she could start on new activities. Tabitha and her dad talked about trying dancing, swimming, reading, and an art class. She couldn't do them all at once, but her dad said that by doing two things, she would add a lot of stuff to her time, and then, if she didn't like one of them after a certain amount of time, she could try something else. But, if she did like them, they could figure out how to work in another activity.

Reading was something she liked to do when she had some downtime, so Tabitha and her dad

made a promise to make sure that they went to the library every two weeks, so she could have some new books.

After they made a plan for Tabitha to do activities, her dad left to do some things around the house. She ate a snack and planned out what she would say to Tony when he got home.

Tabitha loved Tony and didn't want to say anything to hurt his feelings. She didn't want him to stop doing the things that he liked to do, and she just wanted to spend time with him, too. She was nervous about talking to him. What if he gets mad at her for saying something, or if he just laughed at her? What if he didn't want to spend time with her anymore?

Remembering what her dad said, she shook her head to get rid of all the bad thoughts and questions. She knew that even though butterfly wings were flapping in her belly because she was nervous, they would go away once she started talking to Tony. Right now, she was only nervous because she was waiting for him to come home and have time to talk.

She decided she would draw and then read to keep herself busy.

She drew a dog and cat and named them "Shady" and "Stan" after her family's pets. When she was done drawing and coloring her picture, she realized how much time had passed, and she was surprised. After she put her drawing tools away, she took a quick break and saw that Tony had come home already!

Tabitha was happy to see that her dad was right. When she got involved with activities, time seemed to move much faster.

When she walked into the kitchen, Tony waved to her, but he looked busy at the kitchen table. He had a bunch of pieces and parts surrounding him. Although she didn't want to keep him from his project, she was curious to see what he was doing.

Tabitha's nervousness started rising again, but she went over to talk to him about his project. "Hi, did you have fun at baseball?"

Tony looked up and smiled. "Yeah. It was really cool! I worked pretty hard and practised hitting a baseball to score a run!"

Tabitha enjoyed hearing her brother talk about baseball. She saw how excited he was about hitting the ball, and she found herself getting excited for him. "That's great!" she said. "What are you doing now?"

He looked over all his stuff and said, "I'm putting together a rocket. We are all going to blast them off at our next meeting!"

Tabitha smiled, "That all sounds fun." She bit her lip and said, "Can I help you put it together?"

Tony said, "Sure. I don't know what I'm doing yet, so you'll have to wait around for me to read the instructions."

"I can do that!" Tabitha said. "Tony? I have one more question for you."

"Yeah?" Tony said.

"After you're done with the rocket, I'd like to spend some time together. I know that you're busy, but I want to make sure we always make time to be with each other."

Tony put his arm around her sister's shoulder and hugged her close. "I want that too, Tabitha. I think it's a great idea. Let's make sure we spend time together doing things we both like."

Tabitha smiled and was glad that she talked to Tony. She hugged her brother back and then said, "Well? What do the instructions say?"

Tony beamed, opened the instruction manual, and started reading.

~ ~ ~

No matter where you go in your life, you will still be connected if you are kind to your brother, sister, and others you love. Having a good relationship with your family is important. They know and love you more than you will ever understand. If you feel sad or lonely and miss your brother or sister, all you have to do is reach out and talk to them. They will love and support you no matter what, and talking about your feelings will always make you feel better.

Two Sides of the Same Coin

Competition is an amazing way to push ourselves to do our best in all parts of life. When we compete against someone or a team, it's not the winning or losing that is important. It's the way we play the game. If we can become better because someone else challenges us in a new way, that is the lesson we can take away from the competition. You can ask yourself, "what did I learn? How did I learn it? Did someone help me reach this new understanding?"

Yes, winning is fun, but learning to do something better sticks around with you forever.

Having someone who challenges you in school, at home, or in activities doesn't mean they make you feel bad. Instead, they can be the ones who help lift you up and meet all that is possible! And, what is really cool is that you can help them reach their best selves too!

~ ~ ~

Jaden and Jaime both raised their hands to answer Ms. Hanson's question. The teacher called on Jaime, who smiled at Jaden. She was pleased that the teacher called her over him in class. Jaden shook his head at her and said to himself, "I'll get it next time."

Jaime answered the question, and the class moved on to a new topic. When the teacher asked the next question, she picked Jaden to answer it. Jaden proudly gave the right answer, looked over to Jaime, and smiled.

Ms. Hanson saw that Jaden and Jaime were in a battle for answering the most questions because they wanted to beat each other. She sat down and had the students do silent work before talking to them about a team project coming up. The teacher observed that Jaime and Jaden were the best in the class, and they were both very competitive. When Jaden was on a team in the gym and Jaime was on the other side, they would both make the most points. Both of them liked to win—a lot.

Sometimes, they didn't take it very well when they lost (because it happens). And, sometimes, when they won (which happens a lot), they might get a little too excited about winning, and they may not notice that their excitement makes the other team feel bad about themselves.

It was then Ms. Hanson had an idea to help teach Jaden and Jaime to work together. She knew it is a good idea, even if she wasn't too sure about how it would go. She knew that if Jaden and Jaime

worked together, they would make a great team and learn wonderful things about each other and themselves in the process.

After a few moments, Ms. Hanson stood up and said, "Okay, class. Now we are going to do a project about different countries. You will be in teams of two. Find five pieces of information about your assigned country and create a presentation to give to the class in one week."

Jaden looked over at his friend and gave a thumbs up. He hoped he would be paired up with Nick because he and Nick always had a good time when they were doing homework together.

Jaime looked over at her friend Sidnee. She and Sidnee always did their work after school together and they had worked on several projects, which had always gotten them the highest marks. Jaime crossed her fingers that Ms. Hanson would assign Sidnee and her together for their team. She knew they could make a great presentation.

But that didn't happen. Jaime and Jaden listened as Ms. Hanson called out all the names of the other students. Soon, they realized they might be teamed up. They looked at each other

in shock. Neither knew how it was going to work. They had never worked together, and had only worked to beat one another in sports, in school, and everywhere.

When Ms. Hanson called out the last two students, "Jaime and Jaden," they both looked at her as she said, "you two will be a team. Your country is Italy. I am sure you will come up with something amazing." She smiled at them and pretended to ignore the disbelief written on their faces.

They both responded, "Yes. Ms. Hanson," in respectful voices, but didn't sound the least bit thrilled. Ms. Hanson smiled as she turned away, but Jaime and Jaden didn't see this. It never occurred to them that she had done this very thing on purpose. Neither thought that anything good was going to come from it at all.

~ ~ ~

Jaden and Jaime found each other after class to start putting together a plan for their project.

Jaden was the first one to speak. Although they had always competed against one another, they hadn't talked to each other off the sports field or

out of class. "Hi," Jaden said, "I guess we have to do this project on Italy, huh?"

Jaime nodded. She felt very awkward and realized that she had never been around Jaden when it was just the two of them. She gave a nervous swallow and said, "Yeah. I guess so. I can look up three to five facts on Italy if you'd like to come up with the presentation."

Jaden shrugged. "We could go to the library after school and get a bunch of facts together, then pick the best ones?"

Jaime thought that was a good idea. "I enjoy working at the library," she said. She blew out a breath of relief and then had a new idea. She said, "We could actually meet tomorrow at my house instead. If you'd like to look up some facts on Italy overnight, I can do the same, and we can compare the ones we collect. That way, we can get a bunch of facts and then pick the best ones?"

Jaden nodded, and for a moment it looked to Jaime like he was thinking about something. She waited for him to respond, but nothing came out. Becoming impatient, she was about to prompt him when he finally spoke.

"I think that going to the library is a good idea. Ms. Hanson said we were supposed to work together. If we get all the facts at the library today, then we could get all the pieces to build our presentation tomorrow." Jaden watched Jaime's face as she thought about what he said.

Jaime was a bit annoyed Jaden had changed her plan, but as she thought about it more, she realized he was right. They *were* supposed to work together as a team. "Okay," she said. "I think that is a good idea. I can meet you after school outside the front doors, and we can walk to the library together."

Jaden nodded and responded quickly this time. "Sounds good." Although he was trying to play it cool, he was relieved that Jaime listened to his idea. He thought that maybe working with her on this project wouldn't be so hard after all.

Jaime wasn't so sure. She knew that both of them wanted to get the best grades possible, but she wasn't sure how much listening Jaden was going to do. She was still nervous.

~ ~ ~

After school, Jaden and Jaime walked to the library together, talking more about the project and the presentation. "I think we should both read parts of the presentation," Jaime said, "but I can't figure out why Ms. Hanson picked only five facts for each country. Why wouldn't she have said that we could do six because that way each person would get three facts each?"

Jaden kicked a rock. "I don't think it matters who gets to read the facts."

Jaime said, "Okay, good. Then you can read two facts, and I can read three."

Jaden stopped, "Why?"

"Because you just said you didn't care about it."

"I think we should see what facts there are and then decide. Some facts may be longer than others."

"Well," Jaime said, "I like to plan things out before I start on the project, so I know how and what needs to be worked on. Then I create an outline that is also a checklist."

Jaden smiled. "That's a lot of work."

Jaime stood a little straighter, "So? It's how I keep my grades high and how I do so well on tests." She stopped walking and crossed her arms over her chest. "But how would you even know?"

Jaden shrugged. "I get good grades too. I don't do my work like you do, but I still do well on tests and I've even had higher grades than you sometimes. A lot higher." Jaden looked away before saying, "I just wanted to beat you, that's all."

Jaime shook her head and said, "Well. I just wanted to beat you, too."

Jaden looked back at Jaime with shock. They both wanted the same thing! The thought made them laugh.

They both realized that being competitive would not work if they wanted to get the project done together. When Jaime heard Jaden's response about just wanting to win, Jaime understood they were both working for the same thing. She thought about how silly she was being.

Jaden knew he had been stubborn, and when he heard Jaime was just trying to win as well, his stubbornness faded away. He, too, had realized how silly his need to beat Jaime had become.

When they were done laughing, they set off to go to the library and find some books on Italy. Then, they worked together and combined their ideas.

The next Monday, Jaden and Jaime were the first to go. They made a flag of Italy on a poster board and added six facts about the country. Both had learned some new things and got a perfect score for the project, and even got a bonus point for adding an extra fact.

Jaden and Jaime realized when they worked together, they could get incredible results.

Ms. Hanson smiled at the new friendship. She wouldn't tell them what her plan had been, but she was thrilled to see how well it worked.

Ever since that project, Jaden and Jaime have been best friends and always work together to achieve the very best of themselves.

~ ~ ~

Working together in a team can bring lots of surprises. Every person has strengths and weaknesses to balance out the other person. Learning what the other person is thinking is a great way to understand where they are coming from and help yourself be the best person you want to be.

Danny & Delilah Save the Tree

Nature is an amazing gift that every person on earth has. Some people see that nature is beautiful and kind to us. Other people may not realize

how nature helps them every day. The trees and plants across the world give us clean air to breathe and so many other wonderful things.

Being kind to nature is a great opportunity to be kind to yourself too! When you take care of the things outside, they will give you shade, air, and protection. They will take care of you and those you love too!

What would happen if you saw something outside that was broken? Would you chop it down or try to fix it? Danny and Delilah love nature and want to make sure that it is clean and cared for, for many years to come. They do everything they can, they pick up litter, recycle, and more, but when they come across a sapling that looks as though it has been broken, they aren't sure what to do.

~ ~ ~

"Danny, come on!" Delilah called to her brother, and she couldn't wait to get to the park. Although the skies were turning gray, Delilah wanted to walk through the park's rose garden before the rain came. Her legs were running as fast as they could carry her. She wished she had dropped her backpack off from school, as it weighed her down a little.

Delilah heard Danny's feet running behind her, and she wanted to beat him this time, but he was taller than she was and was one year older, so he had one year more practice of running than she did. And while he ran past her, she pushed herself just a little more to keep up with him.

Together, they met at the rose garden in a tie.

Delilah jumped up and down and shouted to show how excited she was that they tied. Danny, her older brother, just shook his head and said, "That was great, sis. You're getting faster! Next year, you'll be able to run races against a whole bunch of kids!"

Delilah hoped so. She loved to run.

But what she loved more was being outside. The colors were always so bright and vibrant, and the air was always fresh. She and her brother did many things outside because they enjoyed nature so much.

Today, at the rose garden, they walked through the aisles of different colored roses, and she smelled every one she could before the first drop of rain came.

Danny, who always had his camera with him, took pictures of the flowers. He did this because he wanted to get photos with all the different light in them. Danny knew gray clouds would cover up the sun, and the roses might look a little darker because a sunny day had extra light than a cloudy day.

Danny loved photography, he enjoyed taking pictures of nature.

Just as the first drop of rain hit a flower petal in front of him, Danny put his camera away. He called to Delilah and said, "Come on! Grab your book bag, and we have to get home before we get too wet!"

Delilah ran past him with a *swish*! And he laughed as his sister pretended to dart through the raindrops, but then picked up his pace because the rain started coming down harder.

They were lucky because they lived a few houses away from the park, and it didn't take long for them to get where they wanted to go. By the time they made it into the house and placed their school bags down, the rain had grown very heavy, and the wind had picked up.

Their mom came down the hall and said, "Buckle up, kids! It's going to be a big storm. You still get to do your homework, though." She laughed and patted Delilah on the head, who pretended to groan and walked into the kitchen with a few books.

Danny smiled at his mom and said, "I finished my homework at school, but I do have a test to study for. But, first, look what I did!" He pulled out the camera and showed his mom the new flower pictures he got. "See, the roses are shaded differently with the clouds." His mom smiled at him and said, "That is amazing. I love your pictures. You should put them in a contest soon."

Danny liked that idea. He thought about it more as he headed into the kitchen to do some studying for his upcoming test.

~ ~ ~

The next morning, Danny and Delilah woke up, still tired. They didn't get much sleep the night before because the storm had been so fierce. The wind blew hard enough to flicker the lights on and off all night, the rain hit their windows very hard, and the thunder was loud enough to shake the mirrors in their rooms. It was a very loud night.

While they made it to school that day, they saw that a lot of leaves were scattered around their neighborhood, along with many branches that looked as though they had been blown off of all the trees that lined the streets. Delilah bit her lip and worried, "I wonder if the rose garden is okay?"

Danny said, "Me too." Since he was older, he felt like he might know a little more than his sister. He thought that maybe the storm last night would have damaged all the roses and hoped that he was wrong. Danny said, "Maybe we should go over after school today to see?"

Delilah agreed. Although she wanted to visit the garden right now, she knew she couldn't be late for school. "When class is over, we will go."

"Sounds like a plan," Danny responded, inwardly hoping that the day would go by quickly.

~ ~ ~

Danny and Delilah were overjoyed to find that the rose garden was pretty clean. There were lots of leaves in this area, but the park employees had cleaned them away from the roses when the kids got there.

"Thank goodness!" Delilah said, hugging her brother. She was very relieved that there was no damage.

"Yes! But look at that, Delilah," Danny said.

Delilah looked to where he was pointing and was surprised to see a small tree, smaller than her, had fallen over. They ran to it and noticed the branches were cracked and a big gash had gone down the small trunk. "Oh no!" Delilah moaned, "We should take this tree home to mom. She'll know what to do!"

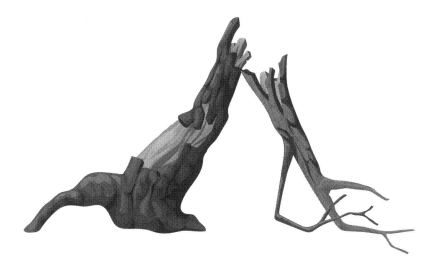

Since the tree was already knocked over, Danny picked it up without digging the roots out. It was a baby tree and was not heavy, but because of the crack in the middle, Danny wanted to be extra careful not to break it further.

When the kids got home, they ran into the house to find their mom. They found her working in her study, and while they knew better than to disturb her while she was busy, they both figured that this could not wait.

Seeing the tree, their mom came out in the kitchen to look at it.

"Ah," she said, "This tree is very young. It's called a 'sapling'."

"Can we help it?" Delilah asked.

"Yes, we can. But we are going to have to hurry. This size tree needs to be in the ground to get water and nutrients to help it grow and heal. Luckily, trees are very resilient."

"What does 'resilient' mean, mom?" Danny asked. He liked to know definitions.

"It means that although it is hurt, it will heal again. It will be different and changed from getting broken, but it can keep living if we take proper care of it. First, we have to get some special tape to tie the cracked part back together. Right now, let's get a few scrap cloths, and we can tie it up. Next, Delilah, can you please wet a few good-sized paper cloths to wrap around the roots?"

Delilah did as her mom asked.

"Then, we'll have to pull all the broken branches off of the tree. Broken branches can take energy from the tree that it needs to heal..." Their mom continued to give instructions, and in no time, the

sapling was tied up, cleaned up, and they were getting ready to plant it in their backyard.

"Let's plant it a little ways away from other trees so it has lots of room to grow and can soak up as much water as it needs it to."

Over the next hour, Delilah, Danny, and their mom planted the broken tree and put up a little fence around it to keep out anyone from mowing it over. The fence also helped it to stand in case of another storm.

Throughout the next few weeks, Danny and Delilah watered the tree when it needed to be wet and cleaned off any falling parts. Danny also took pictures of it. Every other day, he would come outside and take a photo of the tree. He could soon see how the tree was healing by looking at older images he took and comparing them to newer ones.

After some time, they could take the ties off of the tree because the trunk had grown back together. It took a while, but their love and guidance for the tree helped the tree live and thrive.

By the time Danny was ready to move out of their family home and start university, the tree was taller

than their house. Danny had continued to take pictures of it every week while he was growing up and when he looked back on them, he could see how much caring for one tree had helped it live.

Danny and Delilah loved nature even more. They were dedicated to helping it thrive and making a wonderful world for everyone to live in.

~ ~ ~

Nature needs to be taken care of, just like people and other creatures. Learning how to be kind to nature can bring you amazing life experiences, lessons, and an understanding of the world.

Oliva Gets a New Neighbor

Did you ever feel very excited to meet someone but found out they didn't seem as happy to meet you? Did you ask them why?

When you discover the real reason someone acts the way they do, you will realize that they are feeling other things than what you are and that it has nothing to do with you at all! Sometimes the best friends can be made from these situations.

See what happens with Oliva and Johnny when they meet and discover how Oliva makes a new friend.

~ ~ ~

Oliva is excited about dinner tonight. Her parents invited over the new neighbors, and they have a son who is the same age. Oliva always wanted a friend next door, and she hoped that she and the new boy would hit it off.

When she hears the doorbell ring, she runs down the stairs to stand next to her brother and sisters and say 'hello' to the new family.

Oliva's parents open the door, and they all come in. While the adults talk to one another, Oliva walks past her family and says, "Hi! I'm Oliva. My mom says we are in the same grade. I'm excited to meet you."

But, the boy put his hands into his pockets, looked down to the ground, and did not look as happy as Oliva felt. He mumbled, "Hi. I'm Johnny." And he walked past her into their kitchen. He followed close behind his parents, Oliva observed. *Maybe he was shy*, she thought.

But, Oliva didn't let shyness stop her. While she didn't want to make him feel uncomfortable, she wanted to get to know him, so she made a plan to

sit next to him at dinner and see if he would talk to her.

They were eating outside, and when they all walked out onto the porch, Oliva could see Johnny's eyes light up at the sight of their play area. They had swings, a slide, and a wall they could climb on. She went over and said, "Want to go play until dinner?"

Johnny hid his excitement and said, "Yeah. I guess," with less enthusiasm than his face said. Oliva ran over, but she saw that Johnny didn't seem to be in much of a hurry. She wondered why he was trying to hide his curiosity about the play area and fig- ured she would have to find out. Oliva kept run- ning and jumped into the air, grabbing the metal bar in front of her and doing a backflip to look at him upside down.

"Do you know how to do backflips on bars?" She asked.

"No."

"Do you want me to show you how?"

Johnny raised his eyebrows. He was surprised that Oliva wanted to show him how to do something

so cool. He didn't think that his family's move to a new state would make him any friends, but Oliva seemed very nice. Plus, he wanted to learn how to do the flip.

"Okay," He said, although he was still a little uncertain.

She grabbed the bar and lifted herself. Then, she slowly went through the motions.

Johnny was impressed at how she could move and said, "Wow. You're strong," despite his initial hesitation to have fun. He watched Oliva do the flip. As she landed on her feet, she stood up, flipping her hair back over her head. She said, "Thanks! Now it's your turn!"

Johnny stepped up and took hold of the bar. He listened carefully to Oliva's instructions because, in the beginning, she said, "You have to be careful. If you fall, you can hurt yourself. I don't want that, and I'm sure you don't either."

Johnny was grateful she had warned him because he didn't want to fall or get hurt.

As he went through the instructions Oliva was giving, he realized how easy it was to do the flip and was happy to try it. His feet landed on the ground, and Oliva clapped her hands, "Great job!" she said.

"Thanks! I had never thought of doing something like that," although Johnny had seen other kids do it, he hadn't thought to ask them. He was starting to believe that Oliva was not only very nice but helpful and very smart too.

"You did great. Now you can do it faster if you'd like. Or, we can go get something to eat, and you can tell me about the other place you used to live in."

Johnny was pretty hungry, but the thought of talking about where he lived before made him a little sad. Oliva saw his face fell a little when she brought up his other home, so she said, "Or, you don't have to tell me about it until you are ready." Johnny looked up and smiled with relief. He was again surprised by Oliva, "It's okay," he said, "It's just a sad topic. I would like to tell you about it."

So the two ran off to grab some food, and while they ate, Johnny told Oliva that he was unhappy with the move because he had really good friends at his old house. He liked his teacher this year, and he had never lived in any other place before, so moving to a completely new state was not only scary, but it was not comfortable.

"I can imagine," Oliva said, looking up at her house, "I've never lived anywhere else either. I don't think I would like to move at first. But, once I got used to the new place and made a few new friends, it might not be so bad." She bit into her hamburger and chewed thoughtfully.

Johnny nodded, "I didn't think I would meet any-one. I was pretty mad at my parents for moving us." He looked down at his plate, "Even though it wasn't their fault. My dad's work transferred him, and the choice was to either stay in our old house but be without our dad for a little while or move with him. I'm happy that we moved with him."

Johnny looked at Oliva, "I'm glad I met you too!" He said.

"Thanks!" Oliva said, "I was really excited that you were the same age as me and that we were go-ing to be neighbors. I'm glad you told me about your feelings and hope that we can continue to be friends for a long time."

And Johnny agreed. Although he missed his friends back in his old state, he was excited and surprised to make a new friend in Oliva. He hoped that as long as they lived next door to one another (and maybe even if they didn't live next door to each other) that they would continue to be friends.

~ ~ ~

Always remember that just because someone is mad, sad, or angry doesn't mean that you have done anything wrong. Most times, people are just looking for a friend and need someone to understand their side of the story. Johnny was sad because he had left everything he had known. Oliva didn't know that at first, but by knowing his sadness and hesitation were not about her, she opened the door for friendship. When she listened to his problems, he understood that she cared in a new and special way.

Sara the Truth-Teller vs. Kyle the Exaggerator

Telling the truth is always a good thing. Being creative is a good thing too! But sometimes, when you tell the truth do you know if you're saying what is really true or is it just your opinion of what is true?

Opinions are how you think about something. Sometimes, your opinion won't match the truth and sometimes it is going to differ from other people's. (Not everyone likes to wear the same type of clothes, right?) However, when you are extra creative with telling the truth, you run the risk of telling

lies or having people not believe what you have to say.

There is a delicate balance that we have to strike when it comes to talking with people and telling the truth. It's important to realize that not everyone sees the world how you do and that everyone's views are just as important as yours.

~ ~ ~

In class, Sara listened to the teacher's lesson. But she got distracted easily. Sometimes, when the teacher talked too much about a certain subject or a subject that she thought was a bit boring, Sara would start to daydream about other things. Only, her parents had told her she was robbing herself of important things that her teacher was telling her when she daydreamed.

Sara didn't want to let her parents down, so she raised her hand. The teacher, Miss Kensington, saw Sara's hand and said, "Yes, Sara? Do you have a question?"

"No," Sara said. She always liked to tell the truth, "The subject is boring. I am having trouble concentrating. Can you move on to a new topic?"

Miss Kensington smiled, although she was shocked by Sara's admission, she was used to Sara's very honest conversation. "No, Sara. I will not switch subjects. Try to pay attention and please refrain from sharing your opinion with the whole class. It is disruptive."

Sara set her lips in a firm line. She didn't like what her teacher had to say to her, but she wanted to do well in class, so she said, "Okay. I will try harder, but I would rather we moved onto a different subject."

Although Sara liked to tell the truth, she had been talked to by many grown-ups who always said to her she needed to say the truth differently. These grown-ups (including her mom and dad) had told her several times she was disrespectful when she spoke in certain ways. Still, Sara didn't know how to do anything differently, and she continued to struggle with the idea of an opinion and the truth.

Kyle raised his hand and said, "Miss Kensington, maybe if you taught the subjects with sound effects it would be easier for Sara to pay attention?" Kyle was trying to be helpful, but he noticed that Miss Kensington flinched at his suggestion. Although he knew it was a good one, it didn't seem like his teacher would take the idea seriously.

At lunch, Kyle was mad that the teacher didn't like his advice, and Sara was confused about how she was supposed to tell the truth. Everyone always said that telling the truth was the right thing to do. Sara believed that. But what she couldn't understand was how what she said would be considered disrespectful.

Kyle noticed that Sara looked uneasy, and he went to sit down next to her. "What's wrong?" Kyle asked.

"I don't understand about what I said today?" Sara said. "How was what I said today not a good thing? How was I disrupting the class?"

Kyle tossed an orange into the air and said, "I dunno. Maybe it's because you said that the teacher couldn't teach."

Sara sighed, "I didn't say that."

"Yes, you did," Kyle said as he sat up a little straighter. He looked at her and said, "You stood up and pushed your chair back and said, 'Maybe you should teach better, so we all don't fall asleep!' then you slammed your chair back into its spot and slid back into the chair."

Sara got furious. "That is NOT what happened, Kyle. You exaggerate too much!"

"I do not!" Kyle shouted back.

"You do too."

A lunchroom monitor came over to see why they were yelling at one another, "Sara, Kyle—you should keep your voices down. Just because you are eating lunch doesn't mean that you can yell."

Sara looked at the monitor and said, "He is LYING about me."

Kyle shook his head and said, "No, I'm not. I came over to see if you were okay, and you started throwing your food at me."

"I did not!" Sara said. She pointed to the table, "Where is the food if I was throwing it at you? It would be all over the place."

The lunch monitor could see that they would need a teacher to talk to them. So, she said, "You two need to separate and sit at different tables. After lunch, you'll have to talk to Miss Kensington about what happened."

Sara looked at Kyle and said, "Great. Now you've gotten me in trouble."

Kyle shrugged. He couldn't think of anything to say.

After they ate, they went down to speak to Miss Kensington. She saw the two students together and let out a long sigh.

"The monitor tells me we all have a little problem," Miss Kensington didn't wait for them to respond. "Well, I have something that will help you out. Both of you will spend the rest of the afternoon next to

one another. You will act as though you are the other person. If I call on Kyle," she pointed at Sara, "Sara, you will answer in how you think Kyle would respond. Kyle, you will give answers that you believe only Sara would say."

"I don't see how this will help," Sara said. She still didn't see what the problem was.

"Sara," Miss Kensington knelt beside her, "We have a minor issue with the truth between the two of you. Doing this will help you understand how other people see your actions and words." Miss Kensington smiled, "That is if you pay attention." She stood up as the other students came into the class.

Sara watched her teacher with curiosity and wondered how the afternoon would play out.

In class, Sara had to pretend to be Kyle, and Kyle now had to pretend to be Sara. Kyle got the first opportunity to do so, and when he raised his hand to speak, he was very honest, "The answer is forty-six, but in all honesty," Kyle turned to smile at Sara, "We already learned this lesson last year, and I am not sure why we are going over it again."

Sara was shocked that Kyle would say something like that to a teacher. It was obviously for review, but then she realized she had just said something similar to Miss Kensington earlier today. Wow, she thought, *I never realized how telling the truth like that would sound.* Sara now understood what Miss Kensington was saying about how being honest and sharing her opinion were two different things. She hoped Kyle would learn the same thing!

Later in the day the class began an assignment for reading. The class read a story together about a family who got stuck in a snowstorm. When Miss Kensington asked a question Sara thought she could answer with Kyle's exaggerated tone, Sara raised her hand.

"Well," Sara started and had to think hard on how to exaggerate the most out of the answer, "The fire in the story blew out of control because the witch was too angry."

"Sara, there was no witch in the story," Miss Kensington said.

"Yeah, the girl who was the main character. She started the fire because of the ice that was raining down on them for ten days."

"The family was stuck in a snow storm. There was no ice. It was a blizzard."

"But they were stuck forever."

"You just said they were stuck for ten days."

"But ten days probably felt like forever to them," Sara said, realizing now how Kyle saw things differently than she did. He colored his answers with more energy than she did. She looked over to Kyle and saw that he looked as shocked as she felt when he answered in her "honest" way. They smiled at each other.

They both realized that they could use their words to talk clearly. Sara saw how opinion and honesty were separate. Kyle saw that by exaggerating, he was not getting to the truth, which helps people understand how you're speaking and what you mean when talking.

They both turned to Miss Kensington and waved a "Thank you!" to their teacher. They were glad that she helped them see the truth about themselves.

Kyle and Sara still spent the rest of the day answering questions and talking like the other, as

Miss Kensington suggested, and each time they did, they learned a little more about themselves and a little more about the other person.

After that day, Kyle stopped exaggerating and instead used his creative mind to write stories. Sara found a place to share her opinion at the school debate club, and she still told the truth but knew to state her views differently.

~ ~ ~

Remember that honesty can come with compassion and kindness, and bending the truth for any reason can confuse and be harmful for friendships. Learning how to tell the truth with sincerity and understanding was the way to build better relationships with others, including family and friends.

Natalie & Nate
Find the Cat

Things in the neighborhood you live in may always seem the same, whether you live on a quiet street or a busy one. But, knowing what is there and seeing that something is different is always a good trait. Being observant and asking questions helps your brain stay active and gives you a great opportunity to learn things every day. Having a curi-

ous mind is great! Keep your eyes open, and you'll continue to find new wonders.

~ ~ ~

Nate and Natalie live next door to each other. Not much happens in their neighborhood, although they both like living there. They live on a quiet street that can get a little rowdy in the summer for the block party, but every other week tends to be the same.

Each day they get on the bus at the same place. Cars from different houses leave each morning at the same time and come back home later that night. Dinner is always on the table at 6:00 for Natalie and 6:30 for Nate. Sometimes they visit each other's family homes for a meal, and others eat without each other. However, Natalie and Nate spend a lot of time together.

They are very best friends, and they became that way because they both loved to explore and have adventures. Sometimes they would pretend they were spies. Other times they would pretend they were detectives. One thing that they had most in common was that they liked to ask questions and solve problems.

One day after school, Nate and Natalie were playing outside when they realized they hadn't seen the neighborhood cat, Matilda.

Matilda was a little gray tabby cat that didn't live in anyone's house but came to visit them all for warmth, food, and belly rubs. Every day after school, Matilda would find Nate and Natalie and beg for treats. Matilda would also play with them. When they realized that the gray cat hadn't been around today, Natalie started to worry. Then Nate said, "She hasn't been around for a few days, actually."

"Oh no! Is that true?" Natalie thought back for the past few days. She was sad she didn't remember not seeing Matilda. "I feel terrible."

"Me too," said Nate. "Maybe we should look for her."

"Maybe she is being held captive somewhere, or something bad happened to her!"

"Natalie, don't freak out. We can do this, and we can find out where she is. I promise she'll be safe."

"I don't think you can promise that," Natalie said smiling, "But I appreciate you trying to make me feel better."

Natalie and Nate started by walking up and down the street. They were very careful to check behind trees and under bushes. If they saw a neighbor outside or working in their yard, they would ask them if they saw Matilda around. No one had.

Other kids in the neighborhood joined Natalie and Nate on their hunt for the cat. Since no one had seen her, they were all becoming worried. Finally, after looking for what seemed like FOREVER and getting nowhere, Natalie stopped the group of kids and said, "Okay. We need a plan. We know Matilda never goes far from our neighborhood because we love and care for her. Where haven't we looked? What haven't we done? Should we break up into groups?"

"Breaking into groups is a good idea!" One red-headed boy with blue glasses said.

"Okay, then let's break up into three groups," Natalie instructed. Each group had four kids in them. "Group One can knock on doors and ask the grown-ups to check in their garages and sheds,"

Natalie knew Matilda would come into their garage when it rained and thought that maybe the cat would go into other people's as well.

"Group Two, keep looking around gardens, fences, under bushes, and more. Stay in people's front yards and don't go into the back yards unless you get permission—we don't want to be rude. Group Three, you're with me. We're going to explore the woods at the edge of our street. I know there are a few shelter spots that maybe she is in."

Nate stopped everyone before they left, "Come on, everyone. Let's put our hands in a circle for good luck!" The kids stood in a circle, put one hand on top of another one, and Nate said, "Find Matilda on three! One, two, three!"

The entire group of kids shouted, "Find Matilda!" all at once. Yelling got the kids more excited and energized to find the cat quickly. They broke apart, and all went running in different directions.

Natalie and Nate were delighted that so many kids were curious about Matilda. She was a very beloved neighborhood cat.

As Natalie headed down to the woods with her group, she slowed. She didn't want to miss any clues that Matilda the cat may have left.

Natalie looked very closely at the path into the woods and saw a favorite toy given to the cat by her and her brother. The toy was a little mouse, and although it had a dirt on it, it appeared it was just put there recently. Natalie could tell because the toy was on top of fallen leaves, not underneath them.

"Look!" She pointed to the fuzzy toy, "There is the mouse we gave Matilda for a holiday present! She carries that around in her mouth a lot. I think we are on the right path."

They followed the path into the woods and walked slowly. Now that the kids were so excited from seeing the first clue. They wanted to find others.

"Do you hear that?" Another little girl said. She stopped walking and said, "Shhhh... everyone. Stop moving. I think I hear a cat meowing!"

All the other kids in their group froze and listened, trying to hear what the other girl had. Sure enough, they heard a soft meow, meow, meow coming down the hill and over to the left.

Natalie smiled at her group; she put her fingers to her lips to stay quiet while they were walking toward the cat sound. "Let's be really careful. If Matilda is hurt, we don't want to scare her. We'll walk slowly up the hill and see if we can hear her calls still."

Even though Natalie was excited, she tried to contain it because she knew that animals are easily scared if they are snuck upon. And she wanted to help Matilda out, especially if she was injured.

Group Three could hear the cat's calls grow louder. Natalie knew this meant they were getting closer to where Matilda would be. When they came to

the top of the hill, Natalie saw an old wooden dog-house. Matilda's cries were coming from there.

Natalie and the other kids walked up to the house and knelt to find that Matilda was indeed in the old doghouse, but she was not alone!

In the doghouse were four newborn kittens with their eyes still closed.

Natalie put her hand up to her mouth in awe. "She must have just had kittens!" The little ones were still wet and had the softest mew's the group of kids had ever heard. They all said "Aww" together because they were so happy to find Matilda and then were in love with her four newborn babies.

Natalie stood up, she had to go get her dad to help. The kittens and Matilda would need some place warm while they grew up a little. Natalie didn't want anything happening to the kittens and knew that night still got cold even though it was Spring.

"Can you guys keep an eye on Matilda and her kit-tens? I'm going to get my dad to see what we can do with them." The other kids nodded, and Natalie ran to get her dad.

Soon after, groups One and Two heard of the newborns. They all came over to see them. Natalie and her dad returned too.

Natalie's dad carried a box with a soft-looking blanket inside.

Although he shooed the kids away from the doghouse, Natalie and Nate watched on a little more closely. They saw Natalie's dad coax Matilda into the box, but she didn't get in right away. Instead, she carried each kitten out of her hiding place and put them into the box with the blanket one at a time. After all four kittens were in the box, she sat down and looked up at Natalie's dad with anticipation. He smiled at her and said, "very good, Matilda. I'll put you in the box now."

"Why didn't she just jump in?" Natalie asked, curious.

"Because she is probably still sore from having kittens."

"Oh! That makes sense!" Natalie was glad she asked the question.

After a long search and journey, the kids were glad that they found Matilda and that she would be safe and sound. Over the next few weeks, the mother and her kittens roamed around Natalie's house and Nate was over all the time. They all began to build an even deeper connection with the cats.

Their parents agreed that while five cats were way too many for them to have in the house, Nate and Natalie could each have one kitten. But the others would be adopted out to families on their street.

Plus, when the kittens were old enough to be apart from their mom, Matilda wanted to go back outside since she didn't just have one home in the neighborhood. She had all of them.

Nate and Natalie were delighted to each pick a cat to keep as a pet. Nate named his cat Patches and Natalie named her cat Peaches because of its color, and both were very excited that all the cats could grow up together in the neighborhood, and they would never have to be separated from their family.

~ ~ ~

Being curious is a great way to be. When you are curious, you look for answers to questions. You can find clues that will help you solve mysteries and puzzles. They will come with great outcomes too! Every time you find solutions, you learn something new, and then it helps you grow into an amazing person! A little curiosity can always lead to something unexpected, like finding newborn kittens with your favorite cat.

Stella Learns a Lesson

Sometimes it can be hard to make a decision, and other times, it hard to voice what you want. There are moments when you'll need to stand up for yourself and what you believe. When you stand up for yourself and make choices based on what you want, you're telling the world that you deserve your thoughts and feelings to be heard. And you DO deserve to share your feelings and thoughts. The problem may be finding out how to do that with kindness and compassion. But the amazing thing is that you CAN.

~ ~ ~

Stella and Sam met in kindergarten. They were instant friends, both loved superheroes, climbing trees, and eating macaroni and cheese, and they spend a lot of time together. Sam is very loud, enjoys talking, and makes decisions easily. Stella is more cautious about her choices, and she is quiet and sometimes has issues saying what she wants.

Although they always played things that both children enjoyed, Sam stopped asking Stella what she wanted to do after a while because her response was always the same. She always said, "I don't know."

When they entered the new school year, Sam and Stella found they were not in the same class. It was the first time Stella had been with a new teacher, and new students and Sam had not been with her. Stella was nervous about raising her hand in class, giving answers, or even making new friends.

Sam did not have the same problem; he actually made a few new friends in his class, and during the

break after lunch, he started playing with them. Stella got sad that Sam hadn't waited for her to do things too, but instead of saying anything, she just sat alone and watched the other students play on the playground.

When Stella's older sister, Freya, saw her sitting alone looking sad, she went over to Stella and said, "Hi! What's going on?"

Stella mumbled, "Nothing."

"Well, that sounds like something," Freya said, and she sat down next to her sister.

"Sam just left. He ran out with other kids and didn't wait to play with me or ask me if I wanted to come with them. I am lonely, and I am sad."

"That doesn't sound like Sam."

Stella shrugged, "Sometimes he forgets about me."

"I don't think that he forgets about you, Stella. You guys have always been stuck together. Do you think that he just assumed that you didn't want to do something with his new group of friends?"

Stella shrugged again, "He didn't even ask me."

"But what is your first answer when he asks you things?"

Stella looked at Freya and thought for a moment, "I say 'I don't know.'"

"Right. And maybe he didn't want to make you feel uncomfortable by asking you to do something you were unsure of. AND, by the way," Freya smiled, "you can make new friends too. It doesn't have to just be you and Sam as friends. You can still be friends with him and be friends with other people. I think you should talk to him about it."

Stella got nervous at that suggestion. She didn't want to hurt Sam's feelings. But as she looked out the play area and saw the kids running around together without her, she also didn't want to sit by herself, and she knew Freya wouldn't stay with her all the time either. "I'm a little nervous about talking to him," Stella said.

"That's okay. Remember what dad always says about being nervous?"

The sisters smiled together and said, "Just because you're nervous doesn't mean you shouldn't do it. When you are nervous, it means you care. If you're nervous, it means you should do it, anyway!"

Stella nodded. She wished she was a little braver like Freya or Sam, but she hugged her sister and said, "Thank you for making me feel better."

"You're welcome."

"I will talk to Sam about my feelings on our walk home from school."

Freya nodded, stood, and went to play. She left Stella sitting by the tree, where she had begun thinking about how she could talk to Sam about her feelings but remain kind and not get mad or too sad that he played with other friends today.

Stella saw that Sam looked thrilled playing with new friends and didn't want to take away that opportunity for him. Then she thought about what her sister said—that she could make new friends too—Stella worried that she was a little quiet, but also knew that if Sam liked her and Freya liked her, other kids could like her too.

So, Stella planned out what she would say to Sam, and then she made another plan to make at least one new friend tomorrow. With that in mind, she stood up and went back into her classroom as the break after lunch was over.

Sam was waiting for her after school to walk home. Stella smiled at Sam, happy to see that he remembered their daily routine.

"Hi!" Sam said, "I missed you in class today."

Stella pulled her backpack onto both shoulders and said, "I missed you too. I saw you playing with the other kids after lunch." She took a deep inhale and then said, "I was a little surprised when you didn't ask me to play with you guys."

Sam stopped walking and looked at Stella, he frowned, and his eyebrows rose a little. Stella

stopped walking and stood next to him. She waited for him to say something.

He ran his hand through his hair and was clearly nervous about responding. To make him feel better, Stella said, "It's okay, please say what you want to say. I'm happy you made new friends, I just thought you would introduce me to them too."

"I'm sorry, Stella, I didn't think that you would want to play with new kids. I thought... I didn't mean to hurt your feelings."

"I know."

"Do you want to play with us tomorrow?" Sam asked, and they continued walking.

"Maybe. I might try to make a new friend from my class too. Maybe we can all play together?"

"That sounds like a great idea!" Sam said, "Thank you for talking with me about your feelings. I like it when you do that. Although, I am surprised you did. You're always so worried about everyone else's feelings. It's nice to see that you spoke up for yourself too!"

Stella smiled and said, "Freya helped me realize that I should tell you my feelings because they are important. I just didn't want to hurt your feelings and think I didn't want you making new friends. Because I do!" Stella knew that the more people there were to give them love and have fun with was better for everyone.

"That's great! Want me to give you some pointers on how to make a friend tomorrow?" Sam asked.

Stella laughed, "No, thank you, though! I think I'll make a friend my own way and watch you make friends your way. I'll keep talking to you about my feelings from here on out."

"Okay, that's a deal. I'll talk to you about my feelings too."

Stella loved that idea and nodded her head. Being honest with Sam felt very brave. Stella overcame her nervousness and talked to him about her feelings. She was very proud of her actions. She was happy that she could talk to Sam nicely and still respect her feelings. Stella was also very excited about making a new friend tomorrow, and she was excited to meet all of Sam's friends too.

~ ~ ~

Being assertive doesn't mean using harsh words or being loud. Being assertive gives you a voice with compassion and empathy, so you can always be kind and have compassion.

Finn Makes Mistakes

Did you know that you get a chance to learn something new when you make a mistake? Making mistakes may feel strange when they happen—like when you spill water because you weren't holding onto the glass the right way—but, when you make a mistake, you have the chance to see where you went wrong, and then you can fix it for next time.

Next time you hold a glass, you can make sure you pick it up in the right way. Every day, each one of us makes many mistakes, and each time we do we can all look at them as a lesson. Mistakes are never bad things that happen, even if they feel bad.

~ ~ ~

Finn was nervous about his new school, and when he was scared, he knew that he sometimes made mistakes, which embarrassed him. He didn't want to be embarrassed in front of new people, and his belly hurt just thinking about it.

"It's going to be okay," Finn's mom said. She placed a comforting hand on his shoulder and squeezed it just a little. "Try to eat some breakfast, and your belly will feel better."

Finn smiled at his mom. She almost always knew what he was thinking. They were very close. "What if I say something wrong or trip over my feet? When I get nervous..." His mom held up her hand for him to stop speaking and said, "We all make mistakes, especially when we get nervous. No one is going to hold it against you. Just do what you do at home if you trip over your feet. Laugh it off. There is nothing you can say that is *wrong*, you are a very smart boy."

Finn nodded his head, and while he knew his mom's words were very wise, butterflies still fluttered around in his belly.

He ate a little breakfast, and it helped the nervousness settle a little bit, which made him grateful that his mom gave him that advice, but as she dropped him off at his new school and he walked through the door, he tripped over the step leading into the building.

Although heat rose up into his face, he remembered what his mom said about laughing it off. He heard someone else laughing, and Finn turned to follow the noise. The girl wasn't looking his way, and in fact, he realized no one had even seen him trip. He blew out a sigh of relief and kept walking to his classroom.

When he got to the room, he watched the other kids putting away their jackets and book bags in little cubbies on the wall. Instead of following what they were doing, he walked over to the teacher's desk and cleared his throat. When the teacher looked up at him, she smiled a kind smile and said, "Hello! You must be Finn. It's nice to meet you. I am Miss Barley, and I am excited to have you in my class."

Finn nodded his head, and the nervousness crept over his chest and into his face. It seemed like he was a bit frozen and was trying to talk but couldn't. He took a deep breath in and let it out. "I-I am Finn," his voice came out in a whisper, and he was very embarrassed that he couldn't talk at his normal level, but the teacher didn't seem to mind.

She gave him a few books and said, "Why don't you go sit next to Angel? I've told her all about you, and she is looking forward to being your buddy this week. She is going to show you around the school and answer any questions that you have if I am not around." Miss Barley pointed over to an empty desk next to a blonde-haired girl, who waved and gave a big toothy smile.

"Hi! I'm Angel," the girl said when Finn sat down next to her, "You must be Finn! I'm excited to meet you. Stick with me today, and I'll show you the ropes."

Finn gave her a shy smile and nodded. "Hello," he whispered, her enthusiasm made him forget a little more about making mistakes, and he said, "I will. Thank you!" with a little more confidence. The rest of the day, Finn stuck with Angel, and he watched her with some amazement.

He saw her drop her lunch tray and bow when the kids laughed at her. He saw her trip over her un-tied shoelaces. She shook her head, bent over, and tied them up again as nothing happened at all. Finn watched as she raised her hand in class and got the answer wrong to several questions, and he realized that Angel didn't seem to get nervous about getting the answers incorrect. He saw that if she thought something, she would try. That really impressed Finn.

"Wow," he said to Angel as they got ready to leave school, "You really do things differently than I do."

"What do you mean?" Angel asked.

"Well, I was nervous all day today about giving the wrong answers, dropping things, tripping, and more. I think it's great how you just let everything roll over you, and you just keep trying."

Angel smiled and said, "Thanks! Yeah, I'm a bit of a clumsy person, and I learned that as long as I'm going to make mistakes like tripping or dropping, there is no reason to be embarrassed, you know?

I have a lot of other things about me that make me great, and if I am going to make a mistake, that will give me a chance to learn something new about myself."

Finn raised his eyebrows, "I'm glad that you're my buddy this week!"

"I'm glad you're my buddy too. I had never been a student buddy for someone new, and I was nervous about doing it, but you are very nice and kind."

"Thanks! I am learning so much from you. I'm going to learn from my mistakes too. That's a great way to look at life. Thank you for sharing your ideas with me."

"You're welcome!"

The rest of the week went well for Finn and Angel. Each time he made a mistake, said a wrong answer, or came across something he didn't know, he looked at it as a new challenge to learn something. He was happy in his new school and was excited about the new way he looked at life.

~ ~ ~

Every time you make a mistake, you have a chance to learn. Mistakes are great ways to see where things may have gone wrong and change it to do something in a new way. Keep moving forward no matter what challenges you face, and you will find the best experiences even when you aren't looking for them.

A Day at the Beach

Did you ever see something that looked fun to do? Did you want to try it out? What happened when you tried to do something new? Did you find it was easier or harder than it looked? If it was harder, did you keep trying to do it so you could learn how, or did you think about giving up?

We only hurt ourselves when we give up. Not everything in life is going to be easy to accomplish,

but practicing each task makes each experience better.

~ ~ ~

Michael and Katharine are brother and sister. Everybody calls Michael, Michael, and everyone calls Katharine "Kit." Their family loves to travel to the beach. They even have a tiny house there that they go to every summer. They spend the summer months at the house so they can all play in the ocean, build sandcastles, and fall asleep to the sound of the waves.

Although their parents still worked, Michael and Kit were part of a large family and were always surrounded by someone, especially when they went to the beach.

On one windy day, they walked to the beach with their older brothers. After they set up their towels, umbrellas, and cooler, they put sunscreen on and ran out to the water to splash and play. Michael looked down the beach and saw people flying kites. "Look, Kit! That is amazing!" He had seen kites before, but it wasn't until he saw them flying high and mighty that he realized how badly he wanted to fly one himself.

"Let's go ask Brandon if we can go get some kites!" Kit said. Although she usually did what Michael wanted to do (he was older than she was), she thought the kites looked pretty flying in the sky.

Brandon took his younger brother and sister down to where the kites were flying.

There were a ton of kites to pick from. Some of them were cube-shaped, some were snake-shaped, there were even kites that looked like animal shapes. The person selling them explained they should pick out the diamond-shaped kites if they were beginners because those were the easiest to fly.

While Kit and Michael were a little disappointed not to pick out the fun-shaped kites, they were excited to pick out their special colors.

Michael picked out an orange and blue diamond-shaped kite with three green tails on it, and Kit picked the diamond-shaped kite that was purple with a pattern of turtles on it. Her kite only had two tails, but she didn't mind. She knew it wasn't a competition with Michael.

After Brandon paid for the kites, they walked back to the beach. There, they had to tie the strings onto the kites, and both Michael and Kit found that there were two handles for their kites.

"What are these for?" asked Michael. He wasn't prepared to have so many pieces to go with the kites.

Brandon picked up the instructions and read them out loud. "These are called 'fighter kites.' The two handles for the kite will help you move your kite left or right and help it do tricks."

"Wow!" Kit said. She was even more excited about the kite she chose. "Let's get them flying!"

But flying the kites was not so easy.

Each time Kit ran, trying to get her kite up in the air to make the wind catch it, it would dive into the sand. She tried this for a while. Although she wanted to give up, she was determined to get it flying.

Michael was having a different problem. He could get his kite flying in the wind, but soon after, the kite would start spiraling, and the strings would tangle together. Then his kite would crash to the ground. He spent more time unknotting the kite strings than he did with the kite in the air.

Brandon and their other brother, Sean, came over to Michael and Kit. They could see that their younger brother and sister were getting frustrated with the process, and they didn't want them to give up.

Brandon went over to Michael and said, "You have to hold your strings tighter. It looks like you're letting too much slack out. I'll hold the kite, and you say when, and when I toss it up, just unravel the strings."

Michael nodded. Even though he was annoyed with the kite, he knew that if he kept trying, it would pay off.

Sean went over to Kit and said, "Hi! I'm going to help you. I think you need two people for the kite. Instead of running to get the kite to fly, I'll hold it up and toss it. Then, I'll help you with the strings."

Kit said, "Okay! I want to see the kite fly!"

"I know you do!"

Sean held the kite up, and Kit yelled, "Now!" He tossed it in the air and the wind swept the purple diamond shape up and up some more. Kit shouted with excitement but didn't let go of her strings.

Michael and Brandon took a few more times to get Michael's kite flying, but soon, all four kids had the two kites in the air.

Michael and Kit were proud of themselves for not giving up on the kites, and they were grateful to their brothers for offering their help. Having Brandon and Sean help made all the difference. They realized that sometimes they could not do things alone.

They all learned a valuable lesson that day and enjoyed flying their kites for the rest of the summer.

~ ~ ~

Let nothing stop you from completing your goals no matter what challenges you come across. No matter how big or small, if you believe in it, you can achieve it.

Epilogue

And now our tales are over for this time. Do you feel inspired? Do you understand that you can accomplish anything? All the characters in our books are based on you, happy reader. You are unique and have wonderful traits. You are curious, smart, determined, loved, and can do anything you set your mind to.

Remember, the more you practice, the better you'll be! When you have a goal, keep working at it. When you have a feeling, remember to share it. You deserve the best life!

Bonuses
Our Gifts For You

Subscribe to our Newsletter and receive these free materials

Scan Me

www.specialartbooks.com/free-materials/

Stay Connected with Us

Instagram: @specialart_coloring
Facebook Group: Special Art - Kids Entertainment
Website: www.specialartbooks.com

Impressum

For questions, feedback, and suggestions:

support@specialartbooks.com

Nadia Ross, Special Art

Copyright © 2022

www.specialartbooks.com

Images by © Shutterstock

Cover Illustration realized by
Maria Francesca Perifano

Made in United States
Troutdale, OR
11/04/2024

24431556R00062